WITHDRAWN

D0603166

BUD
and
Gabby

MONTEREY COUNTY FREE

SALINAS
CALIFORNIA

LIBRARIES

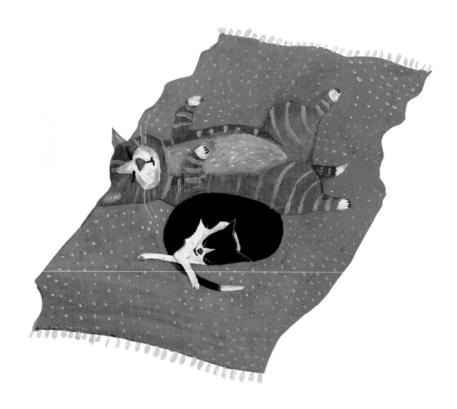

For Joe and Kathryn

Bud and Gabby
Copyright © 2006 by Anne Davis
Manufactured in China.
All rights reserved. No part of this book may be used or reproduced in any
manner whatsoever without written permission except in the case of brief
quotations embodied in critical articles and reviews. For information address
HarperCollins Children's Books, a division of HarperCollins Publishers, 1350
Avenue of the Americas, New York, NY 10019.
www.harperchildrens.com

Library of Congress Cataloging-in-Publication Data
Davis, Anne, date.   Bud and Gabby / by Anne Davis.— 1st ed.   p.   cm.
Summary: Bud the cat becomes very worried when his feline friend Gabby
gets sick and finds a special way to show his friendship when she returns
from a visit to the veterinarian.
ISBN-10: 0-06-075350-1 (trade bdg.) — ISBN-10: 0-06-075351-X (lib. bdg.)
ISBN-13: 978-0-06-075350-4 (trade bdg.) — ISBN-13: 978-0-06-075351-1 (lib. bdg.)
[1. Cats—Fiction. 2. Friendship—Fiction.] I. Title.
PZ7.D285546Bud 2006   2005015145   [E]—dc22

Design by Stephanie Bart-Horvath
1 2 3 4 5 6 7 8 9 10
❖
First Edition

BUD
and Gabby

Hi

I'm
Bud

This
is
Gabby

words and pictures by **Anne Davis**

HARPERCOLLINS *PUBLISHERS*

I guess I'm the bossy one.
I always get the comfy chair.

Sometimes Gabby's a real pain.

But she is funny.

Our
mornings
are
for
grooming...

and afternoons are for napping.

I like to read with Gabby.

She has an excellent vocabulary.

Sometimes we like to look at things upside down

or really up close.

And we always stick together.

It was just awful when Gabby got sick.

She turned all yellow and hid in a drawer.

I tried to make her laugh.
The only sound she made
was a little snort.

I knew it was serious when I saw the box,

and off she went.

I was so worried
I overgroomed.

As a result,
I got a huge hairball.

She
loves
bugs
and
spiders.

She's not afraid of anything.

And she was teaching me how to knit!

She's very patient.

Besides,
I can't open
the door
without her.

She's back!

She smells kind of like
a medicine chest—
but she looks great.

Her appetite's awesome,

and everything's working okay.

From now on, we share the comfy chair.

WITHD. D0603157

For centuries, children of all cultures have been fascinated by fairy tales. Why do these stories from another time still hold so much interest?

The presence of fairies in these tales is not as important as the fact that the action takes place in worlds far removed from the daily life of a child. The story opens with "once upon a time," allowing the child to enter it without feeling threatened.

Fairy tales depict conflicts that echo universal issues all children encounter. Whether the story deals with ambivalent feelings, rivalry, sexuality, death, or fear of the future, the ending, which is usually happy, offers a solution without lapsing into the morality of fables.

The most important element in a fairy tale is magic, and the central characteristic is magical language. The child is introduced to the creative power of words. Through words, the child plays, explores the world, and soothes troubling tensions. Through the magic of language, a disgusting beast can turn into a handsome young man, an adult may remain imprisoned in a lamp for centuries, or three little pigs may represent three feelings that animate a child. This creative use of language not only makes the story attractive, but also shows children that words have the power to express what they feel, which is sometimes difficult to do. It is not easy for young children to imagine for example that they can hate someone they love. This reality can become more accessible when a loving grandmother turns into a wolf capable of devouring a little girl.

The surreal adventures of fairy tales depict real truths that children may experience, offering a way to face those realities by appealing to the child's imagination. This is why fairy tales are as current today as they ever were.

Martin Pigeon, Psychoanalyst

Beauty And The Beast

Traditional tale
Illustrations: Pierre Brignaud • Coloration: Marcel Depratto

"Caillou, Rosie, it's bedtime," Grandpa called. "Let's go. Put on your pajamas and brush your teeth. Then you can have a story."
Caillou and Rosie didn't waste any time. They loved piling onto Caillou's bed with Grandpa for story time.

"There was once a very rich merchant, who had three beautiful daughters. His youngest was admired not only for her looks but for her goodness and everybody called her Beauty, which made her very mean and very vain sisters very jealous indeed.

One day, the merchant lost his entire fortune, except for a small country house at a great distance from town. He told his children, with tears in his eyes, that they most go there and work for their living. The two eldest answered that they would never leave the town to raise sheep in the country!

Beauty was sad at first. "But," she said to herself. "If I cried, that would not make things any better. I must try to make myself happy without a fortune." She could not think of ever leaving her father.

When they came to their country house, the merchant applied himself to farming and plowing the fields, and Beauty rose before daybreak to clean the chicken coop and ready the meals for the family. The good merchant knew very well that Beauty outshone her sisters, and admired her humility, industry, and patience, for her sisters not only left her all the work to do, but insulted her every moment.

One morning, the merchant received a letter stating that a vessel on which he had merchandise had safely arrived. This news excited the two eldest daughters, who immediately begged him to buy them new gowns, ribbons, and all manner of trifles.

"What will you have, Beauty?" asked her father.
"Since you have the goodness to think of me," she answered,
be so kind as to bring me a rose."
Once in town, the good merchant went to court about the
merchandise, and after a great deal of trouble and pains to
no purpose, he went back as poor as before.

The merchant was within thirty miles of his own house, when going through a large forest, he got lost. Night was coming on, and he began to think he would either starve to death with cold and hunger, or else be devoured by the wolves, which he heard howling all around him.

He saw lights at some distance coming from a palace at the end of a long walk of trees. The merchant hastened to the palace. He entered into a large hall, where he found a good fire, and a table plentifully set out. He waited, and still no one came.

At last he was so hungry that he could stay no longer, but took some chicken, and ate it in two mouthfuls.

After this, he walked the halls until he came into a chamber, which had an exceedingly good bed in it, and he thought it was best to simply shut the door, and go to bed.

The next morning the merchant awoke, and he looked through a window, but instead of snow, he saw the most delightful gardens, with the most beautiful flowers that ever were. He was also astonished to see a good suit of clothes in the room instead of his own.

As he left the castle, the merchant passed a bed of roses and he remembered Beauty's request to him. He gently picked one and immediately he heard a great noise, and saw such a frightful beast coming towards him that he was ready to faint away.

"You are very ungrateful," said the Beast to him, in a terrible voice. "I have saved your life by receiving you into my castle, and, in return, you steal my roses, which I value beyond anything in the world. You shall die for it."

"My lord," said the merchant. "I beg you to forgive me, I had no intention to offend in taking a rose for one of my daughters, who desired me to bring her one."

"I am not a lord," replied the monster, "but the Beast. I will forgive you, on condition that one of your daughters comes willingly and suffers for you. Go, but swear that if your daughter refuses to die in your stead, you will return within three months."

The merchant had no mind to sacrifice his daughters to this monster, so he promised, upon oath, that he would return. He then left the castle and in a few hours he was home. His children came round him.

"Here, Beauty," said the merchant. "Take this rose, but little do you know how dear it will cost your unhappy father.

He then related his fatal adventure. Immediately the two eldest cried woefully and said all manner of ill-natured things to Beauty.

"See the pride of that little wretch," said they. "She would not ask for fine clothes, as we did, but no, Miss wanted to distinguish herself, so now she will be the death of our poor father."

"Why should I?" answered Beauty. "For my father shall not suffer upon my account. Since the monster will accept one of his daughters, I will deliver myself up to all his fury, and I am very happy in thinking that my death will save my father's life."

The merchant could do nothing to dissuade his dearest daughter from delivering herself to the Beast. The older sisters were themselves delighted and these wicked creatures rubbed their eyes with an onion to force some tears on the day of Beauty's departure.

Towards evening the good man and his daughter saw the palace illuminated at the end of the path. As they entered into the great hall they heard a dreadful noise when the Beast appeared.
The Beast asked Beauty if she came willingly. Beauty was terrified at the Beast's appearance, but she took courage and said, trembling and fighting back her tears, "Ye-e-s."
The merchant, all in tears, then bid his poor child farewell.

"Beauty," said the Beast. "May I dine with you?"

"That is as you please," answered Beauty.

"No," replied the Beast. "You are mistress here; you need only bid me gone. But tell me, do you not think me very ugly?"

"That is true," said Beauty. "For I cannot tell a lie, but I believe your heart is good."

"Yes, yes," said the Beast, "my heart is good, but still I am a monster."

Beauty ate her supper, and had almost conquered her dread of the Beast; but she nearly fainted away when he said to her, "Beauty, will you be my wife?"

It was some time before she dared answer, for she was afraid of making him angry, and trembling, she said, "No."

The poor Beast sighed heavily and left the room.

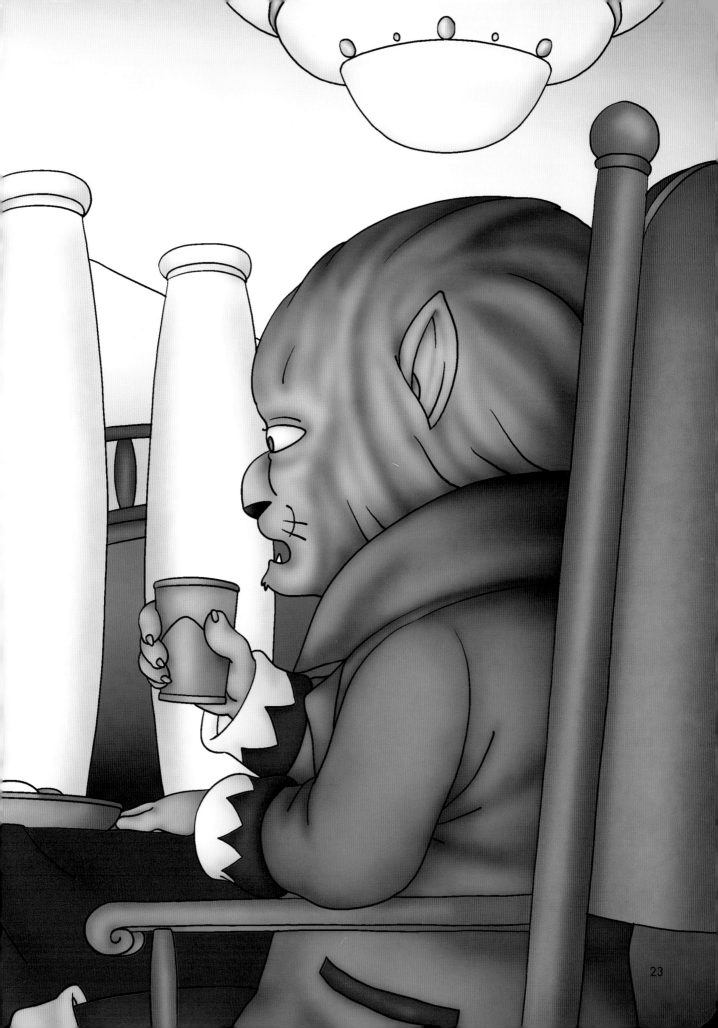

Beauty spent many months in the enchanted palace and seeing the Beast often, had grown accustomed to his deformity. There was but one thing that gave Beauty any concern, which was, that every night, before she went to bed, the Beast always asked her if she would be his wife.

"At least," said the Beast. "Promise never to leave me."

"I could," answered she. "But I have so great a desire to see my father, that I shall worry to death, if you refuse me that satisfaction."

"I will send you to your father. But know this, should you remain with him, then I will die with grief," said the Beast.

"No," said Beauty, weeping. "I promise to return in a week."

"You shall be there tomorrow morning," said the Beast. "You need only lay your ring on a table before you go to bed, when you have a mind to come back."

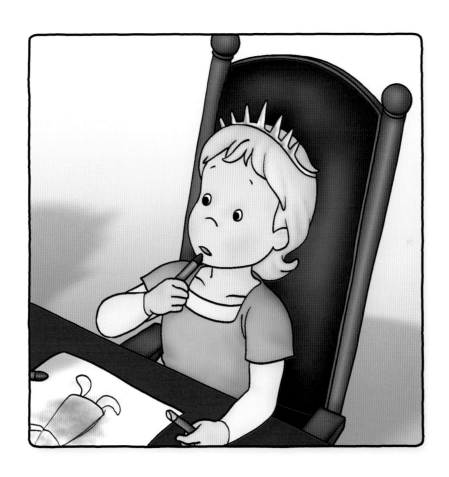

Beauty awoke the next morning at her father's house. Her father was overcome with joy to see his dear daughter again. Beauty's sisters sickened with envy, when they saw her dressed like a princess, and more beautiful than ever. The two conspired to take their revenge by ensuring the monster's wrath and making Beauty remain longer than the agreed time of a week.

The sisters behaved so affectionately to their sister that poor Beauty wept for joy. When the week was expired, they cried and seemed so sorry to part with her, that she promised to stay a week longer. The tenth night, Beauty dreamed she was in the palace garden and that she saw the Beast dying. Beauty woke from her sleep in tears. "I am most wicked," said she, "to act so unkindly to the Beast. It is not his fault that he is disfigured. He is kind and good to me, and that is sufficient." Beauty then put her ring on the table.

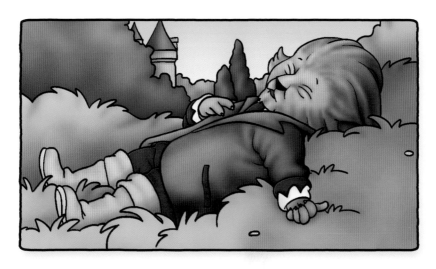

When Beauty woke the next morning, she was overjoyed to find herself in the Beast's palace. She ran out into the garden to where she had dreamed she saw the Beast. There she found poor Beast stretched out, quite senseless, and, as she imagined, dead. She threw herself upon him.

The Beast opened his eyes, and said to Beauty, "You forgot your promise, but since I have the happiness of seeing you once more, I die content."

"No, dear Beast," said Beauty. "You must not die. Live to be my husband. I cannot live without you."

Beauty scarcely had pronounced these words, when she saw that her dear Beast had turned into a handsome prince.

"A wicked fairy had condemned me to remain under that shape until a beautiful girl should consent to marry me. In the whole world, there is only you generous enough to be won by the goodness of my character."

Overjoyed, Beauty gave the charming prince her hand, and they went together into the castle where they were married and lived happily ever after.

© 2012 CHOUETTE PUBLISHING (1987) INC.
All rights reserved. The translation or reproduction of any excerpt of this book in any
manner whatsoever, either electronically or mechanically and, more specifically,
by photocopy and/or microfilm, is forbidden.

CAILLOU is a registered trademark of Chouette Publishing (1987) Inc.

Traditional tale
Consultant: Martin Pigeon, psychoanayst
Illustrations: Pierre Brignaud
Coloration: Marcel Depratto
Art Director: Monique Dupras

The PBS KIDS logo is a registered mark of PBS and is used with permission.

We acknowledge the financial support of the Government of Canada through
the Canada Book Fund for our publishing activities.

Canadian Patrimoine
Heritage canadien

We acknowledge the support of the Ministry of Culture and Communications
of Quebec and SODEC for the publication and promotion of this book.

SODEC
Québec

Bibliothèque et Archives nationales du Québec and Library
and Archives Canada cataloguing in publication

Brignaud, Pierre
[Caillou: la Belle et la bête. English]
Caillou: Beauty and the beast
(Fairy tale series)
Translation of: Caillou: la Belle et la bête.
For children aged 3 and up.

ISBN 978-2-89450-949-4

I. Leprince de Beaumont, Madame (Jeanne-Marie), 1711-1780. Belle et la bête. English.
II. Title. III. Title: Caillou: la Belle et la bête. English. IV. Title: Beauty and the beast.

PS8589.I64C3513 2013   jC843'.6   C2012-940458-6
PS9589.I64C3513 2013

Printed in Guangdong, China
10 9 8 7 6 5 4 3 2 1 CHO1844 JUN2012

3 1901 05384 4413